Jeannette R Clark

Nettie's Poems

Jeannette R Clark

Nettie's Poems

ISBN/EAN: 9783337341855

Printed in Europe, USA, Canada, Australia, Japan

Cover: Foto ©Andreas Hilbeck / pixelio.de

More available books at **www.hansebooks.com**

NETTIE'S POEMS

AND A FARCE:

OLD FOGY AND YOUNG AMERICA.

BY

JEANNETTE R. CLARK.

CINCINNATI:

1880.

CONTENTS.

(iii)

APPENDIX.

OLD FOGY AND YOUNG AMERICA (A FARCE DESIGNED
FOR BEGINNERS OR HOME THEATRICALS.)

POEMS.

CASTLES IN THE AIR.

Oh, 't is bliss and joy to know
We poor mortals here below
Can leave below all want and care,
To dwell in castles in the air.

Oh, what rapture doth it bring—
We 're so happy we can sing ;
Oh, there 's naught on earth so fair
As our castles in the air.

There 's not an emperor, prince, or king
An army strong enough can bring,
To subjugate our castles fair—
Our bright castles in the air.

Do n't tell us we are beggars here ;
We will flourish, never fear.
Do n't talk to us of want or care,
While we 've castles in the air.

No monarch e'er so rich as we;
We from grief and care can flee;
We 've no place for grief or care
In our castles in the air.

Like fair visions in the skies,
Now they fade, again they rise;
How they glow and glitter there—
Our bright castles in the air.

Look above the gloomy cloud;
Here we ring the praises loud.
Oh, what makes our life so fair?
Our bright castles in the air.

COMING OF SPRING.

Sweet Spring came smiling o'er the hills,
And loos'ed the ice-bound rippling rills,
And breathed upon the bare-boughed trees,
Life-giving power lent every breeze.

Sweet Spring came smiling o'er the plain,
Waking germs to life again;

Bright Phœbus kissed each em'rald spear,
And dew-drops hung there like a tear.

And Phœbus drank the dew-drops fair
That sparkled so like diamonds rare;
And day by day he kissed each blade,
And soon sweet flowrets decked the glade.

THE LOST CASCADE.

On a May day as fair as e'er dawned,
  I lingered awhile in a dell,
Where a cascade, all joyous with laughter,
  Came bounding with joy from the fell.
Came bubbling, and springing, and gushing,
  Like a child loos'ed from tyrant's restraint;
Drear Winter had ta'en his departure,
  And its joyousness sure was no feint.
"Ye bright waters, how I long to embrace you,
  Each bubble I would greet with a kiss,
As dancing with rapture they mock me
  With murmur, and laughter, and hiss.
Ho, ho! wanton waters, how gayly
  You flirt on your way to the sea;

Like the belle of the season, you're regal,
  And have the best wishes from me.
Would your waters might sparkle forever,
  A clear little rill by itself;
But, ah, you will mix with strange waters,
  Made useful for barter and pelf.
Your individuality lost—lost forever—
  An atom amid the vast waste.
Then why, sparkling cascade, so joyous?
  Oh, why such unreasonable haste
To a fate so unhonored and somber,
  Engulfed in the waves of the sea?
Oh, who can e'er find thee, my darling,
  To bear thee a message from me?"
Would Old Ocean hear me, I'd tell him
  Of a truant so happy and free,
Just loos'ed from the chains of Old Winter,
  Now lost mid the waves of the sea.
And I'd bid him be tender—so tender—
  To this waif, once so crazy with glee,
That, heedless of warnings and signals,
  Wildly rushed to the arms of the sea.
" Be tender, Old Ocean, and gentle,
  Mid thy waves, rocked forever and aye,
Bear this waif to some calm, blissful haven,
  Where it still may be happy and gay.
And when on thy strands I may wander,

Should a gay, laughing wavelet I see,
I shall know 't is the sprite of our cascade,
Which comes for a greeting from me.

THE BEE AND THE BUTTERFLY.

Said the Bee to the Butterfly, " Beautiful one,
Gorgeously flitting in the Summer day's sun,
Come help me, I pray thee, in the dew-laden bowers,
Gather rich sweets from the blossoming flowers.
I gather rich honey from each tiny cup,
And for cheerless, cold Winter treasure it up.
I will give you a home in my warm, cozy hive,
Where, in the cold Winter, in comfort you 'll thrive.
Without food or shelter, beautiful fly,
When the cold blasts come, you surely will die."

BUTTERFLY.
"Now, silly Bee, I will speak, by your leave.
O'er your direful predictions I shall not grieve.
Could a gay Butterfly, dainty and bright,
Ever be found in so sorry a plight?
And what would my comrades think to see
Me toiling along with a poor humble Bee?

Such drudgery would never become such as I,
And I do not believe I ever shall die.
Such work would soil my gilded wing,
Then what peace would your honey and cozy hive
· bring?"

BEE.

"Yes, yes; you might soil your gauzy wing,
But would save your life, you giddy thing ;
And when the rude storms and cold weather is over,
Again you may flit 'mong the sweet-scented clover."

BUTTERFLY.

"I see you're conceited, Mr. Bee," said the Fly,
"And think you are very much wiser than I;
But I know very well the world's broad and wide,
And when Winter comes here, I will to the other side.
Ere the first frost comes, I will away,
To a clime where flowrets bloom for aye."

So away she flew, the beautiful thing,
Crimson and gold was her glossy wing;
And the Bee toiled on 'mong flowers sweet,
Collecting sweet stores in the Winter to eat.
And when a cold day came, in his hive hid away,
Till dawned a fair, warm sunny day,
Then away would go the busy Bee rover,
To fields where still blossomed the hardy clover.

He roved one day, and sought in vain
For bud or flower on the frost-blighted plain.
Turning sadly back to his cozy retreat,
A sorrowful sight did his wandering gaze meet.
Cold and dead, in a stubble-field of rye,
Lay his beautiful friend, the Butterfly.
Busy Ants were dragging her body away,
To serve them as food on the coming day ;
Her velvety wings, now soiled and torn,
Slowly adown their dungeons were borne.
The giddy fly had wasted her time,
Neglecting to seek the Winterless clime.

MORAL.

From this little story, you the lesson may learn,
The advantages of industry never to spurn.
Those who disdain to do aught but flaunt,
Perhaps at last may die of want.

THE TRUANT ZEPHYR.

A little zephyr, on the wing,
Kissed me—ah, the truant thing ;
Kissed me on the cheek and brow.
Where is that little zephyr now ?

I told her she was sweeter far
Than crescent moon or twinkling star;
She kissed me, and she kissed again—
How could I tell her to refrain?

I called her sweet enchantress—dear delight;
She hugged me in her arms of light;
The matchless charmer I begged desist,
Lest I should perish of pure bliss.

Her airy wings full-fledged with odors rare;   [hair:
The breath of flowers imprisoned in the meshes of her
Her drapery was the sunlight sheen—
Pray who has this sweet zephyr seen?

Flitting through all the sunny hours,
Balmy odors bringing from Flora's rarest bowers,
I would I might imprison her for aye,
That she might near me ever, ever stay.

HOPE.

Hope is sweet, but 't is delusive;
  If budding flowers would always bloom,
Life would be one flowery pathway,
  From the cradle to the tomb.

Hope, sweet Hope, our hearts would break,
　If it was not for thy cheering;
Life would loose its golden hue,
　And our souls be ever fearing.

Hope, sweet Hope, still lend thy cheering;
　Paint the future happy, gay;
What would life be, Hope, without thee?
　Space, without of light a ray.

Drear as an eternity of darkness,
　Sad as an eternity of woe;
Man would wander, sad and cheerless,
　Nor peace nor joy would ever know.

E'en the wretch all bound and fettered,
　In his dismal, iron-bound cell,
Unknown, uncared for, and forsaken,
　Acknowledges thy mighty spell.

E'en the criminal on the gallows,
　Clad in the garb of death,
Life on earth, or life above,
　Hopes for with his latest breath.

POMP AND SIMPLICITY.

A lady reclined in her easy chair,
There were pearls round her neck, and gems in her hair;
Her velvet robe was made with care,
  And wrought with threads of gold.

I should not murmur the fate, said she,
Which makes me a lady of high degree;
But pomp and show have no charms for me,
  And my simple heart yearns for my humble home.

This palace grand is no home for me;
I long to roam, unfettered and free,
My native mount, where the lonely bee
  Probes the mountain floweret.

I, bred a simple rustic maid,
Shall ever love the woodland shade,
The towering mount, and lonely glade,
  More than gilded palaces.

Decked in gems, like a princess I dwell,
A blighted flower, a stranded shell,
Yearning the old home I love so well,
  Though rustic and humble it be.

What care I for wealth or fame?
What care I for a titled name?
What care I for a wide domain?
　These for the gaudy proud.

Gold to me seems glaring and bold;
Diamonds to me have a glitter that's cold;
Emeralds I love with a love grown old;
　But the grass-green turf is sweetest emerald to me.

For sapphire gems, what care I?
Let me gaze on the blue of the azure sky;
Not gems nor gold my heart can buy,
　Nor entice from its humble love.

I love the rock-bound ocean shore—
Perhaps the rugged mountain more,
Where the cataract leaps with a rush and roar,
　And, murmuring, flows to the valley below.

Fashion shall not, with her thousand snares,
Lure me to bind with her million cares;
Before she chains me unawares,
　I will ward off her coils and be free.

Take the glowing gems from my glossy hair;　[care;
Take the gold-broidered robe which was wrought with

Take all the wealth and grandeur I share—
  While I hie me away to my rustic home.

I shall sing sweet songs in my cottage home ;
Never again shall I wish to roam ;
The rippling rill, with its bubbles and foam,
  Shall soothe and comfort me.

Bring now the swiftest, sprightliest steed ;
Away, away, o'er the flowery mead,
Swift as the wild winds, now we speed
  To my mountain home away.

Come see my cot on the mountain set,
Like a cozy nest in a leafy net,
Mid the greenwood gleaming like a minaret,
  Or a star in the dome of heaven.

Come see my pasture, with its flock of sheep ;
Come see the old well, with its weather-brown sweep ;
Come see the fields where the reapers reap
  The ripened, golden grain.

Come see my table, all snowy white,
Where gayly the sunbeams, warm and bright,
Through vine-wreathed casements, airy and light,
  Cast flickering shadows o'er platter and bowl.

Come list the music of birds and bees;
Come list the wild winds among the trees;
There's naught on earth more soothing than these—
   Nature's sweetest melodies.

Then farewell for aye to the stately dome,
Where pomp usurps the pleasures of home;
O'er all the earth, wheresoe'er I roam,
   I found naught to my heart like my own cot home.

LESSONS FROM NATURE.

When sorrows cluster round thee,
   And cares obstruct thy way,
Oh, turn not to the cruel world—
   Her lessons lead astray.
Go rather to the wild flower
   That blooms by the wayside fair,
On the rugged, thorny pathway,
   Neath God's protecting care;
Or to the stranded gem
   That on the beach is thrown,
Which, till the tempest wave upheaved,
   In beauty lay unknown;

Or to the little violet
    That buds and blooms unseen,
In the tangled wildwood,
    'Neath the coppice green ;
Or to the tiny seed·
    Dropped by the birds in air
Upon the desert oasis,
    To bud and flourish there.
Thus sweetly are we taught
    To put our trust in God—
To trust in His protection,
    Though 'neath the chastening rod.

THE BARBER OF CADIZ.

There was a handsome lady ;
    She was very fine to see ;
She lived at No. 80,
    In the city, near the quay.

She wore such stylish dresses,
    And had such a queenly air,
And looked so consequential,
    And withal so debonair.

She set her sails to marry,
  But said no common brute,
Nor nothing less a knight or lord,
  Her exquisite taste would suit.

Peers are not so very common
  In our democratic nation,
And she waited, year by year,
  For a lordly declaration.

She watched the ships from Europe,
  And sped to Saratoga,
Enveloped in her graces,
  Like a Roman in his toga.

She waited year by year;
  The while was growing older;
While a wrinkle here and there,
  Of youth's evanescence told her.

A wag of Saratoga town,
  Growing wild at her rejection
Of his impassioned suit,
  Planned revenge in his dejection.

Not far from Saratoga town
  Lived the barber of Cadiz,

A lordly looking fellow,
　With a very handsome phiz.

Our wag told the handsome barber
　How a lady fine and gay
Was waiting for a lord to come
　Some thousand miles away.

You are a true lord of creation,
　You barber of Cadiz,
With a very lordly physique,
　And a fine patrician phiz.

Go win this peerless lady,
　And all expenses I will pay
Of finger rings and other things
　To hymen's bands the way.

This barber was a trifling flirt;
　That is, he understood the art
Of flinging cupid's arrows,
　While he dodged every dart.

So nothing loth he started,
　With a golden-headed cane,
His borrowed coat and breeches,
　And his very little brain.

He the supercilious fair one sought,
   With his pompous airs and graces,
Strutting like a turkey-cock
   In his most lordly paces.

Birds of a feather flock together.
   So soon, alas! they meet,
And our snob, a la Parisienne,
   Falls sniveling at her feet.

Like a true knight, he knelt before her;
   Vowed his heart she did ensnare,
In the glances of her bright eyes,
   In the meshes of her hair.

"A wandering peer from Europe,
   Lonely from home and friends,
Sadly thy favor would entreat
   For all thou makest amends."

Thou fillest the void in mine aching heart.
   To thee I pay my vows;
My heart is thine, if thou 'lt be mine.
   None but thee would I espouse."

" Oh, 't is fate!" cries she; "I know thee!
   I have met thee in my dreams;

Lord, I am thine, and thou art mine;
  My heart with rapture teems."

So they were married by and by,
    And he took her to Cadiz,
Where skillfully he plied the art—
    The shaving of the phiz!

At this, she cried, " What do I see!
    You blessed lord of lofty station,
Thus waiting on the common herd,
    In such an occupation."

" I fear thou art deceived, my dear ;
    I am one of the many ' lords of creation,'
Who earn their bread and butter
    By every occupation."

Pitying, he loved, consoled her ;
    Many years have passed away,
And lordly barbers multiply
    In fair Cadiz to day.

DICK AND BETTY.

Betty was our bard,
And was not skilled in mixing lard,
And flour, and eggs, and meal,
Nor aught that goes to make a fancy meal.
She could sing a song,
Or trip the light, fantastic toe;
But cook a deft dinner?   Our Betty?   No!
Poor Betty!   Many ups and downs she had;
She fell in love with a ragged lad,
And straightway to a priest did go,
And they were married so and so.
Poor Betty!   What was wealth to a noble heart?
What was poverty to Cupid's dart?
Alas, alas!   it came to pass,
Poor Betty sighed, and cried, and dreamed,
And Dick dug, and delved, and steamed.
Alack-a-day!   hard was the way
Of honest Dick and dreaming Betty.
Betty sought the hidden treasure;
Dick measured taters, measure after measure.
  Betty whiled away the leisure moments,
    Building castles in the air;
  Dick replenished the empty larder,
    Catching rabbits in a snare.

Poor Dick !   Poor Betty !
Time grew apace, and Dick grew lean,
And Betty's sunny smiles were seldom seen.
Time grew apace, and so their family grew,
And children now they numbered two ;
Two little cherubs to scold and pet,
Named Dickey boy and baby Bet.
Poor Betty made them mush and slush to eat,
And taught them how the great grandees to meet.
Poor Dick, he noted they their clothes outgrew,
And sighed the wherewith to buy them new.

Poor Dick !   Poor Betty !
The weary years they flew and flew ;
The darling cherubs grew and grew.
But Dicky boy was mamma's pride,
And baby Bet should be a rich man's bride.
But papa made poor Dickey hoe the corn,
Till set of sun, from early morn.

Poor Dickey !
Mamma taught him how to walk erect,
With dignity and self-respect ;
Papa learnt him how to dig pertaters,
And, cobbler-like, to mend his mamma's gaiters.

Poor Dickey !
Baby Betty grew, and mamma curled her hair,
And, with a look of pride, praised her little princess air.

Papa bought a scrubbing-brush, and taught her how to
   scrub ;
Mamma sat and wept to see the little creature rub.
Poor baby Bet, she sighed ; is this your fate—
To rub and scrub, and pine and fret ?
Ah, we shall see ; it shall not be !
She knelt her there and made a vow
That baby Bet and Dickey boy
Should have some play, should have some joy ;
That poverty should not enchain
Her ever-scheming, dreaming brain.
Wealth and ease and joy to gain,
To work she put her witty brain.
In fiction, poesy, and art,
She soon assumed a busy part.
Full soon the world her genius knew—
Success her gift of plenty threw ;
And baby Bet. and Dickey boy,
And Dick and Betty had joy without alloy.

CHEERFULNESS IN ADVERSITY.

On the bending bough of a leafless tree,
  On a cold December day,

A sweet bird sang a song in glee,
　As cheerily as in May.

The barren earth, in its icy mail,
　No shelter gave the lonely bird;
Yet far away, o'er hill and dale,
　Its cheerful notes of joy were heard.

I listened the song of the warbling bird,
　And it breathed not a note of sorrow;
But sweetest notes of joy were heard,
　As it cheerfully sang of the morrow.

Sweet bird, thou a lesson of wisdom hast taught,
　In adversity's hour through the gloom look afar;
Beyond may be found a bright future, if sought.
　Dark clouds and mists hide many a bright star.

PATSEY CASEY.

" I'me Patsey Casey, your honors,
　Fresh from the Imrald Isle;
And me Irish heart is thumpin'
　Like a drum beat all the while.

" For me heart is slashed and broken.
    If you'le listen to me tale—
.I know your heart's in sympathy—
    My sorrows will bewail.

" I will tell ye's of the times agone,
    Across the waters wide,
Whin I was young and handsome,
    Wid Patherick by me side.

·"Ah! thim were darlin' times we had,
    And Patherick loved me so ;
And he was the swatest gallant
    That iver I did know.

"And he sid my eyes were brighter
    Than ony eyes that blinked ;
And wid joy our hearts were tipsy
    Whin heart to heart was linked.

"And, oh ! Patherick was so swate on me ;
    Sure he brought me ribbons rare
To tie aback my purpled locks
    Of Irish blue-black hair.

"And I was swate on Patherick, too :
    How could I hilp it now ?

Was n't he the natest gintleman
That iver made a bow ?

" Was n't his two eyes the keenest
    That iver pierced a sowl ?
And his blarney tongue the lurinist
    I iver ran afoul.

" Will, thin, I'de fling tin thousand chaps
    Across the Irish sea,
If by this act I might succeed
    In kapeing Pat wid me.

" But now the saddest story comes :
    How Patherick took to drink ;
How the de'il wint in and Pat wint out,
    I can not bear to think.

" How the divil changed my Patherick dear,
    Till no speck of him were left,
And I looked around to find me
    Of ivery joy bereft.

" 'Twas whisky stole my Patherick,
    And left a beastly looking sot.
I might tell of countless throubles,
    But I think I 'd rather not.

" For that was the onlikeliest cut of all,
    That stole me handsome Pat,
And left a bloated iffigy ;
    The deil give this for that.

" Oh, Patherick ! Patherick ! loved and lost,
    My bleeding heart would leap wid joy,
Could I recall thee as thou wast,
    My once noble, noble boy."

Enter Patherick, reformed.
    " Ho, Patsey ! darlin of me heart,
    To thee I vow the sacrid vow
That never again shall rum enchain,
    Nor rob thee of my heart of hearts.

" I threw the foaming schooner down,
    I tossed the wine cup in the air ;
And never again shall drink enchain,
    If you my love and life will share."

They join hands and sing in concert.
    " Drink, drink, never more think
    Our lives again to sever ;
One we shall be, while we are free
    From rum's vile bondage ever.

THE POET'S FANCY.

A poet once, in his garret old,
  His chimerical brain in fanciful play,
Imagined himself a monarch bold,
  And his garret a palace gay.
His rickety chair, that would scarcely stand up,
  He fancied a chair of state;
Sat himself there, clad in purple and gold,
  With a crown on his grizzled old pate.
Cobwebs, that dangled from rafters above,
  And in festoons low at his feet,
He admired as ancient tapestries,
  With gem adornings replete.
His hungry old cat, wauling for food,
  He thought was music grand;
Listening in rapture profoundest,
  As if to an orchestra band.
As louder it wauled, the gayer he smiled;
  "Encore!" he shouted, "Encore!"
Till the rickety old mansion echoed
  From garret to cellar floor.
He did very well till he thought to dine,
  As dine all monarchs should;
He gazed at the cupboard, empty and bare
  Of aught resembling food.

There were empty dishes, cruets and bowls,
But nothing like food, but some old rusty jowls.
He was hungry, e'en as his hungry old cat ;
And longed for a roast, rich, seasoned and fat.
He earnestly gazed at the empty wine flask,
His chimerical brain was not up to the task.
" My kingdom," he cried, " my kingdom and crown
For a nice roast of beef, rich, seasoned and brown."
He sprang from his chair, stamped wildly the floor,
For the fanciful dream of the poet was o'er.

THE TEA-KETTLE'S SONG.

How soothing the song the tea-kettle sings,
As o'er the flaming fire it swings ;
How peaceful the sight of the broad glowing hearth,
The warm cosy kitchen, where it sings in its mirth.

We recall the home picture, again and again,
Where the tea-kettle sings as it swings on the crane ;
Now it whisper's and moans where the red fire gleams,
Telling wierd-like tales as it sputters and steams.

Drowsily we list to the sweet tale it tells;
Now it rings a gay cadence, like soft tinkling bells :

Now murmers in sadness, now laughs as in glee;
Oh, wierd-like indeed are its murmurings to me!

Ah, a magical thing is the tea-kettle's song;
We smile and we sigh as it rumbles along,
Rousing memories most sweet as it whispers and sings,
While scenes from the past to life it brings.

CATCHING A FLEA.

If you want to catch a flea, nab him, grab him;
  Don't try to catch him by the tail,
  He don't travel like a snail,
  You can't sight him like a whale,
  He's like a wiggler in a pail.
And if you want to nab him, grab him!
  You must take him by surprise,
  Grab him, head and tail, eyes;
  When to get away he tries,
  Tightly pinch his little thighs.
Then, if you think you've got him,
  Do not venture a sly peep,
  Or he's sure to take a leap,
  And will bite you in your sleep,
    This little monster flea.

Rub him hard and rub him fast,
He is growing weak at last,
His fleaship's biting days are past,
He has bit his very last,
　This trifling little flea!
Put him lightly on the floor,
Stamp him once or twice, or more,
And the annoying little bore
Will bite again no more.
Sure as fate he's got away!
Where did he go? you say.
Must have gone the other way.
The vile insect would not stay
　Till you stamped him on the floor.
If again you see that flea, nab him, grab him!

THE LIGHT-HOUSE KEEPER'S DAUGHTER.

I am the light-house keeper's daughter,
　I live beside the sea,
And 'tis said I'm smart and pretty,
　And I hope this true may be.
But I've a trouble hard to bear;
　Every year I'm growing older,

And I never had a sweetheart,
  And the beaux seem growing colder.
I winked at Johnny Bliss—
  Do n't you tell my mother—
Might as well have winked at Jupiter,
  Or at my baby brother.
He turned and looked at me, and says :
  "You 're growing saucy, Sade."
And oh ! if somebody do n't marry me soon,
  I shall live and die a maid, I shall live and die a maid !

I called at Peter Penelope's ;
  He keeps the hardware store.
He talked to me of hatchets, screws,
  And other hardware lore.
My smiles were all in vain,
  My best wit was thrown away ;
He only talked of picks, rakes and scythes,
  Through all my lengthened stay.
He showed me irons and pokers,
  Knives and forks all in a row.
Throw your forks away, Pete Penelope ;
  And your knives all in a row,
Would be about as useful
  As a girl without a beau.
He looked askance at me, and said :
  Is not that rather pointed, Sade ?

And oh! if some one do n't marry me soon,
  I shall live and die a maid, I shall live and die a maid;

I called at Brown's the baker's;
  He looked so fine and gay,
I thought it was a pity a bachelor he should stay.
  Mr. Brown, said I, have you a wedding cake.
No, said he, that is a thing we very seldom bake.
  If you want a wedding cake, said he,
I 'll give to you a recipe;
  First, butter, eggs, and sugar white,
These you must have to make it right.
  No, Brown, says I, that can not be,
I know a better recipe.
  Common cakes are made of butter, eggs and spices;
But *wedding* cakes, dear Brown,
  Are always made with *lasses.*
I am a lass myself, and so I ought to know;
  You can not have a wedding cake,
Without a lass and beau.
  Says he, my goodness, gracious!
I hope you 're not a hintin', Sade?
  And oh! if some one do n't marry me soon,
I shall live and die a maid, I shall live and die a maid!

LIFE AND YOUTH.

Youth.

Haste, life with thy treasures,
Time is fleeing away;
Haste, haste, with the joys
Ye have promised so long.
Oh wildly I covet the joys ye withhold,
While youth glides away
And time flies along.
Haste, life, with the chalice,
So temptingly held,
Filled to the brim
With pleasure and joy.
We will drink to the dregs,
A bumper to thee;
The nectar of bliss, unmixed with alloy.

Life.

My pleasures are transient,
My treasures decay;
My joys are like phantoms,
So soon do they fade.
But beyond is a portal
Where life is immortal;

And joy is unceasing
In that heavenly glade.
There let your treasures be;
Time can not corrode them.
There look for pleasures
That fade not away.
Fear God, and be wise;
Love man, and be happy;
Thus lay up a treasure, forever and aye.

LINES TO THE HEARTH FIRE.

Beautiful hearth fire, glowing in light,
Leaping and dancing, as if in delight;
Great is thy power, oh, beautiful fire!
To chase away gloom, hope to inspire.

Always cheering, 'mid wintry glooms,
Is the glowing fire, with its flaming plumes;
Light and warmth, with forked tongues flinging,
Vanquishing cares, while happiness bringing.

Glow, ye red embers; dance, oh, light of flame!
Thy cheer is always and ever the same.
All who have felt the wintry blasts know
The joy that is found where the hearth fires glow.

THE OHIO IN SUMMER.

From a rocky shore I gaze afar
On a river whose waters pelucid are.
" River of beauty," by Indians named :
A river always for beauty famed.

On the glassy breast of this silvery stream
The sky's brightest tints on the waters gleam,
And morning's fair resplendent skies
Paints it with her golden dyes.

When the setting sun unrolls in the west
Her burnished curtain in crimson drest ;
Each roseate hue in the sunset screen,
Mirrored below on the water is seen.

When gentle eve enwraps the earth
And heaven's dome with stars doth girth,
She sees below on the flowing wave
Each twinkling star in beauty lave.

When luna appears, fair queen of night,
Robing earth and sky in her amber light,
The moonbeams on the ripples play
Till the horizon hides each tangent ray.

LINES TO THE EVENING STAR.

Linger awhile in thy beauty,
  Gem of the azure dome ;
Where meteors flash through space,
  In that boundless realm, thy home.
Queen of the eve, thou comest
  When the sunlight falls low,
With a glittering band around thee,
  To shine where the misty clouds flow.
A guide and guard thou seemest,
  A sentinel of the sky.
We hail thy silent watches,
  While the lone stilly hours pass by.
Thine is no menial duty
  To guild the gray shades of night,
With thy gem-like beauty adorning
  Heaven's hall with silvery light.
Thou art a memorial of heaven ;
  For wanderers will, lingering, gaze,
And ask where 's the God of such beauty,
  And bow in humble praise.

THE WILD BIRD'S PRAISE.

A wild bird gaily singing
  Woke me early in the morning,
And I roused me from my slumbers
  To note the bright day's dawning.
Through morning's golden flood gates
  The light was streaming wide ;
Dazzling gleams were peeping
  Through the window by my side.
Chasing Morpheus, the drowsy god,
  From my senses with a will,
I determined I would see
  What made the birds so gay,
As unwearily they carolled
  In the bushes by the way.
As forth I wandered slowly,
  Listening the cheerful lay,
I learned the happy story ;
  It was the warbler's praise of May.
Thus morn had waked in beauty,
  Merry spring brought joys anew ;
Carolling praises was a duty,
  The praise their maker due.
Flowerets exhaled sweet perfume,
  Like diamonds shone the dew,

While Phoebus slowly mounted
　The sky of purest blue.
The anthem sweetly echoed,
　In the dingles by the way ;
Repeated oft the praises
　Of the wild bird's whistled lay.

THE FOUNT OF KNOWLEDGE.

On the road of life is a fountain rare,
　Flowing from Time's eternal stream ;
All pilgrims who have tasted know
　Its waters clear with blessings teem.
In that fountain, calm and lonely,
　Many a blessing may be found ;
And within its hidden depths,
　Gems of beauty vast abound.
Wisdom near that fountain hovers,
　Strewing precious truths around,
For those who drink of waters
　Where such priceless gems abound.

But each anxious wanderer lingering
　Round the fount to win a gem,

Should willing take the task of life,
　　And the stream of error stem.
Then near the fount of knowledge linger,
　　Near the source of wisdom stay,
And see upon each sparkling bubble,
　　Lessons for the coming day.
If sincere, he there will find,
　　Like crystal dew-drops clustering fair,
Many a truth to bless mankind,
　　Luring thoughtful pilgrims there.

In that bright perennial spring,
　　Is rich reward for valiant youth ;
Who quaff the precious waters,
　　To vanquish all that poisons truth.
Such valiant mortals now will see
　　Mystery fade like mist away ;
And dark errors from the past
　　Obstruct the pilgrim's way.
Willing they gird their armor on,
　　To battle for the right,
Dispelling darksome shadows,
　　To give the world more light.

ILE AND GAS.

Isabella Rickets was the belle of Carbon Station,
And Ned the grandest beau that walked
In all this glorious nation.
Her young affections to beguile,
He told her he'd discovered ile. ·
And as the days along did pass,
She told him she'd discovered gas.
As they walked one day the cool piazza,
Locate, said he, your grand bonanza.
She laid her hand upon his head ;
'Tis here, said she, you saucy Ned.
Locate, said she, your well of ile.
Says he, Miss Belle, it was your sm—ile.
So, having neither ile nor gas,
Their lives as one could never pass ;
And, being poor as two pertaters,
They summoned up their pride ;
Ned threw his life away in war,
And Iserbeller Rickets died.

THE GENTLE FROG.

A gentle frog sat on a log,
Singing wog, wog, wog, wog;
A little boy in passing by,
Says "bully frog, what makes you cry?"
Says the frog, "I can but cry,
Cause all my beauty's in my eye."
A man who kept a restaurant,
Whose tables sure, were never scant;
A man who surely ought to know,
Because he loved spring chicken so;
Hearing Sir frog's direful plaint,
To bring him comfort, made a feint.
Cease, said he, that doleful cry I beg,
For though your beauty's in your eye,
Your *sweetness* sure is in your *leg*.

MIRANDA; OR, WORKED TO DEATH.

I was a woebegone bachelor once,
With no wife to caress or love me;
I wandered the green earth over,
And looked at the blue skies above me.

What my talents, I never could tell;
What my mission, I ne'er could divine;
Whether to soar above earth in a balloon,
Or seek nether earth in a mine.
But fate brought a cherub before me,
Her name was Miranda, the darling;
I cared for naught else any more.
I left off my sky searching and snarling,
The balloons shot aloft as before;
The men worked like bees in the mine;
Heaven and earth were naught to me now,
I saw naught but Miranda divine.
I followed, I told her I loved her;
She called me a lout and a fool.
And I thought if I marry Miranda,
She surely, yes surely will rule.
But I would rather have been a mosquito,
Pinched tween her thumb and her finger,
Than be hidden from sight of Miranda,
A heart broken bachelor to linger.
Miranda, dear Miranda, do love me,
I sighed, and I sighed, and I sighed;
At last the sweet creature said yes,
And we were off like a rocket and tied.
I was so blissful I could not but laugh;
Miranda turned up her little pug nose,
And called me a giddy calf.

I bought her some tubs and a stove,
A broom, a brush, and machine.
Now you can work like the dickens you dove,
And make me some puddings I ween.
And some nice ruffled shirts for my best,
And well laundry my vest and my coat,
And have pies for each dinner, my darling,
O'er such luxuries I fondly do gloat.
And I'll bring you some company my dear,
Some friends from the North and the South,
And you'll make us some sweet cakes my dear,
Your cakes bring my heart in my mouth;
And some light fluffy biscuits, Miranda, ·
Such good biscuits as your's were ne'er seen ;
And to make the repasts more genteel,
Some floats and some jellies I ween.
How it was I never could tell,
But Miranda grew crabbed and cross ;
'Tween irons, washtub, and bake-oven,
She flew like a racer almost.
Whoopee! Miranda, my darling, I said,
Your'e a treasure, Miranda my dear.
Keep your knives bright and shiney, Miranda,
And your tin ware like silver clear.
This earth were a desert without you,
I ne'er lived till I wed you my dear ;
But you look slouchy and care worn, Miranda,

Growing slipshod and careless I fear.
But some canvass back duck bake for dinner,
Will you not, Miranda, my dear?
She faintly murmured of duty,
And there coursed down her cheek a bright tear.
Weeping for joy are you, Miranda?
If you're happy as I, well you may;
But I 'do rather you 'do dry up your tears,
And be pert as a girl and as gay.
Pert as a girl and as gay, alas!
Pert as a girl and as gay.
Miranda she weakened and died, poor thing;
Died like a rose in full bloom,
And I planted the beautiful sunflower
Over her marble white tomb;
Over her marble white tomb, alas!
How did it ever come to pass,
That I weep o'er her marble white tomb?

MEMORIES.

There is nothing so cheering,
  To recall as you may,
As a batch of sweet memories,
  Packed nicely away.

To cheer a lone hour,
    There is nothing so sweet
As a page from the past,
    With dear memories replete.

Smiles of absent ones,
    Looks of dear ones passed away,
Kindness of the loved and lost,
    Are gems to be treasured for aye.

The hand that plucked away the thorns,
    And strewed our youthful path with flowers,
Will be treasured in memory forever,
    Till clasped in heaven's bowers.

THE FIRST TEMPTATION.

The wiliest of serpents lay coiled in a tree,
Where luscious fruit hung temptingly.
Lovely Eve beneath the boughs was straying,
With the beauteous buds and blossoms playing.
" This wondrous fruit," said she, " I must not eat."
Like rippling music came reply, " 'T is sweet, 't is very
    sweet."

" From this wondrous tree of knowledge I must fly,
For should I eat, ah, then, I'd surely die."
" Nay, woman, eat, thou shalt not die."
Curious Eve now listens in surprise—
Sinless, pure, what knew she of lies?
" I wonder," are the only words she said ;
To hear the voice again, she bends her sunny head.
Again the wily voice with subtle art replies :
" If thou but taste, oh, lovely Eve, thou shalt be wise ;
That it hath power to kill, I do not deny,
And promise thee thou shalt not surely die."
She, yielding to temptation tastes,
And quickly with an apple hastes
        To Adam.

WHISPERS OF THE BREEZES.

Each whispering breeze tells a different tale ;
They sigh in the woodlands, and sing in the vale.

" What do the breezes say to thee,
    Maiden gay, with the starry eye?
What might the import of their whispering be—
    These little breezes, as they pass you by ? "

MAIDEN.

They tell a sweet, sweet tale of joy;
  They whisper me a future bright,
Of happiness without alloy,
  With every dear delight.

What do the breezes say to thee,
  Ardent youth, in thy strength and pride?
Do they murmuring sigh, or merrily sing,
  As they linger awhile at your side?

YOUTH.

The breezes say, onward, still on;
  They whisper of glory and fame,
And tell me how, on another day's dawn,
  I shall win me a deathless name.

What do the breezes say to thee,
  Woman fair, and sweetly sad?
Do they bring you cheer, in their wanderings free,
  And promise a future joyous and glad?

WOMAN.

Oh, no, no! the breezes, how dreary
  They wail a sad song in mine ear;
Life seems more sad, my heart still more weary,
  As the soft, wailing breezes I hear.

What do the breezes say to thee,
  Man of sorrow, sadly dreaming?
Do they say your cares shall quickly flee,
  Like mists 'neath the warm sun's beaming?

MAN.

Despair, despair, is the cruel air
  Of the breezes that mock my sorrow;
They howl in mine ear, till I languish with care;
  And I can not but dread the morrow.

What do the breezes say to thee,
  Poor old man, with silvery hair?
Do they sing of the golden pasi in glee,
  And paint in thy future times as fair?

OLD MAN.

Peace, peace, say the breezes, in sooth,
  And sing of a haven beyond the sky,
Still as balmy as e'en in the days of my youth,
  Though old age dims the light of mine eye.

ORIGIN OF THE WHITE LILY (*Lilium candidum*).

Blooming fair in a wild wood,
    A bright little wild flower grew,
With pearly leaves gem laden,
    As it peeped from the sward through the dew.

It timidly peeped through the leaflets,
    And murmured a song on the air,
As calling the stray little florets,
    It whispered its thoughts to them there.

And it softly and sweetly whispered,
    As its starry eyes trembled to see ;
The floral beauties appear as it called
    A companion sweet flowers for me.

Then forth came a snowy white lily,
    A wee little tender bloom,
And peeped at the bright-eyed daisy,
    Through clusters of thyme and broom.

Daisy, espying the sweet lily, said :
    " Of all the fair flowers I see,
The snowy, golden-eyed lily,
    Appears the most lovely to me."

Then lily became so elated,
  The companion of daisy to be,
She reared aloft her fair head,
  That all flowers her beauty might see.

Then Flora, the goddess, appearing,
  The pride of the lily did see;
And to punish her vainglorious folly,
  Declared ever tall she must be.

Then lily could never more mingle
  With the sweet humble flowers at her feet,
And daisy, the bell of the wild wood,
  With kisses she never could greet.

WAITING IN FAITH.

Waiting, waiting! Oh, when will the light dawn?
  Sadly I wait in a gloom black as night.
In blindness and darkness I wander, so weary;
  But God is my helper: *He* will guide me aright.

Waiting, waiting! Oh, let me be patient;
  For God is my help: He'll not lead me astray;

While friendless and lonely I wait for the dawning,
  For light and the truth to illumine my way.

For in God do I trust, else I had perished.
  My burden so heavy, so grievous to bear.
Like Peter, I cried, " I perish, Lord save me ;"
  And a promise from God dispelled my despair.

So I am waiting, 'mid sorrows and darkness ;
  By and by a sweet light on my pathway shall shine ;
For God is my friend, and I have His promise,
  And firm in faith, wait His promise divine.

THE DYING SOLDIER.

1 am dying, oh, I 'm dying! and my home is far away.
  I shall see no more that happy throng,
  Nor join again the evening song.   [you pray.
Father, mother ! far away that son now dies for whom

I am dying, oh, I 'm dying ! I would that they were here
  To wipe the death damp from my brow,
  That gathers damp and heavy now.   [parting tear.
Loved ones of home ! ah, none are here to drop for me one

I am dying, oh, I'm dying! They will look for me in vain;
 They will listen for my coming,
 When they hear the distant drumming;
While I lie beneath the sod, and they'll see me not again.

I am dying, oh, I'm dying! If they were only here,
 They would smooth my tangled hair,
 And would breathe for me a prayer.
I crave their loving smiles, my latest breath to cheer.

I am dying, oh, I'm dying! I see a light above,
 I hear the angels singing,
 To me salvation bringing;
They heed the dying soldier. Ah, truly, God is love.

AFLOAT ON LIFE'S BILLOWS.

Afloat on the billows of life,
 With no rudder or compass to guide.
Oh, what do the roaring billows,
 The shrieks of the wild winds betide?
The wayward current, how swift
 Does it bear to breakers below?
Or on to a harbor of peace,

Where placid waters flow ?
The danger and darkness, how dense !
    Death shrieks in each wild hissing wave.
Is there peace on this river of life ?
    Or does peace only come with the grave?
Peaceful isles in the river I see,
    But breakers rush madly between.
Unguided, my bark on the river is tossed ;
    My signal of woe is unseen.
Distress signals loom in the air,
    Many heralds of danger and woe ;
White flags in the track of the maelstrom appear,
    But to sink in abysses below.
Help ! help ! to my fellows I call.
    A wail echoes back on the air ;
The blackness of darkness broods over all ;
    In each heart broods the spirit despair.
Mercy ! mercy ! mercy ! Great God on high,
Heed a poor sinner's despairing cry ;
Stretch forth thine arm, all mighty to save,
And guide our frail bark o'er the treacherous wave.
Grant us courage and faith through the tempest to ride ;
Grant thou our prayer ; be our guard and our guide.

THE DYING GIRL.

Oh, tell me not that I must go;
I love this darling dear earth so.
There may be brighter worlds afar,
But earth is still the loadstone star,
That binds me here with chains of love;
Such chains I know were wrought above.
Then say not 't is a sinful tie;
Such links our earth to heaven on high.
God will not surely chide me so;
He made the earth and all below.
This binding love he gave it birth,
And chained therewith this beauteous earth.
Only an isle afloat from heaven,
By old time storms and tempests riven;
Only an isle cast off by God;
His presence breathes in every sod.
There is no power that e'er can sever
The links that bind us there forever.
The glories of heaven I have not seen,
But many are lent to this old earth green,
And they have bound my heart below,
Till I am loth to leave them so.
I can not easily say farewell,
I love too well this earthly dell.

But what are we but souls afloat,
And earth our tempest driven boat;
And love, the anchor from Heaven cast,
To draw us safely home at last.
For heaven is home, and each soul afloat
On earth our tempest driven boat;
By love of God to Heaven may speed,
By God's love from every blemish freed.
Farewell, farewell, to this beauteous earth ;
Farewell to the home that gave me birth ;
Farewell dear ones here below ;
God's will be the only will I know.
Farewell to all things here I love ;
I seek a holier home above.   Farewell !

DREAMS UNFULFILLED.

I turn to the fleeting years adown time's dark vista,
    And ask them where are my beautiful dreams ;
Did fancy awake them, to fade like the flowers,
    Or pass like the shadows o'er silvery streams ?

They gleamed like sunshine on floral bowers,
    Flashed in the sunlight of beauty awhile,

Then like a snowy cloud fled from my view,
And deigned not again in beauty to smile.

Where are my bright dreams? In memory only
Can I faintly trace the silvery line;
Yet fondly I turn where once they were blooming,
And find light mid the shadows brought by old Time.

TURNED OUT.

"Oh bid me not go;
Stern landlord relent;
The cold is so bitter,
The night winds so wild.
Oh, turn me not out,
My last penny is spent,
I am widowed and orphaned and unwise as a child

"I once had a home more lovely than thine;
Every comfort and luxury then were they mine;
But fortune is fickle.
O, landlord, relent,
And send me not out in the darkness to pine.

" Thy frown—ah, how dreadful—
Crushes hope in my soul.
You will not relent;
God have mercy on thee.
You bid me to hasten ;
Oh, where is the door ?
I will go. You 're a traitor to God and to me.

" Out in the stormy night—
Oh, God ! can it be ?
Homeless and friendless ; ah, where shall I go ?
The world seems so cruel and bitter to me,
As I wander alone through the cold drifting snow.

" On, on, in the darkness ;
I shall perish I know ;
But why should I murmur ?
I ask not to stay,
I wish not to' live,
While friends are so false.
I must kneel in the white crusted snow drifts to pray.

" Oh, Jesus be merciful ;
Thy precepts I love ;
Thou hast wandered as homeless
And friendless as I ;
Thy compassion will pardon.

Oh, hear and forgive,
And admit my poor soul to thy mansion on high.

" Lord, to thee I commit my spirit.
Forgive a poor wanderer,
And take me to rest ;
Thy mansions are many,
And no wintry blast comes
In that beautiful land, the land of the blest.

The morning sun is shining
O'er the cold snow-crusted moor,
And 'mid the deep drifts lying
The form of our wanderer.
Too late, alas, to comfort,
Her weary soul hath fled.
The ice-crusted drifts
Of the cold white snow
Was our wanderer's dying bed.

THE VOYAGE; OR, SUMMER FRIENDS.

Once there lived in a famous town,
A man of wealth, and of renown.
Friends flocked around on every side,

For hospitality was his pride.
" How many friends I have," he cries;
" I can not see them with mine eyes;
Should want or woe e'er come to me,
I shall not want for friends," says he.
" There 's not a man in all the land
That can present a nobler band—
Disinterested, kind, and true,
Each and all will prove true blue."
They came in crowds, they clustered round,
No end of friends could e'er be found;
They ate his meats, and drank his cheer—
Of scarcity they had no fear;
For bounteous tables always stood
Laden with rare and luscious food.
How cheerful in his park to roam;
None ever seemed to long for home,
But lounged about, and lingered there,
As free from want as free from care.
Quoth he, " While here so many friends are found,
Awhile I 'd like to wander round;
More of this world I long to see,
And as I wish so let it be.
Safe wife and children in their hands
1 will intrust, and visit foreign lands."
So, by and by, he bade adieu
To wife and children—friends so true—

Embarked on a staunch ship of the sea,
And steamed away the world to see.
O'er ocean wave, afar, afar,
And then the elements seemed at war ;
Wild tempests swept the ocean wave,
Where tossed the ship of our hero brave ;
The lightnings glared, and thunders crashed,
While furious waves the good ship lashed,
And tossed from wave to deep abyss,
With impetuous roar and raging hiss.
At last she sank to rise no more,
As many a good ship has before.
Our hero clutched a floating spar,
And borne he was afar, afar.
Upon a wild, lone shore, at last,
Weak, worn, and fainting, he was cast,
And happy thus to 'scape a grave
Beneath the wild sea's cruel wave.
A wilderness this friendly shore,
Where wild beasts prowled the forests o'er,
And wilder natives monarchs trod
O'er all this wild though beauteous sod ;
Gem-laden, too, the golden sand
In this fair and sunny land.
With the subtle power which knowledge gave,
He charmed the native warriors grave ;
Thence wandering free their forests o'er,

Or, lingering, watched on the wild sea shore,
Gazing afar for friendly sail—
Oh, happy the hour might he bid one hail.
Thus wearily waiting, year after year,
No word from home to give him cheer ;
Oh, how cruel the wide sea seemed,—
An impassable barrier it ever gleamed
Parting him from friends and home—
Oh, why did he ever wish to roam ?

  * * * * *

A sail ! a sail ! At last ! at last !
A signal high on the winds is cast.
'T is seen ! 't is seen ! Oh, happy sight—
The tilting ship, with sails of white,
Toward the shore her prow doth turn,
Where the beacon light doth burn.
Swift on the flood our hero springs,
And abaft the white-flecked sea foam flings,
As swift he swims, on the rolling tide,
To the gallant vessel's dripping side.
With shouts of cheer he is drawn aloft,
And every sailor's hat is doffed,
While he tells them of his days of woe,
And the happy home of long ago—
Of wife and children dear to his heart,
And many friends from so long apart ;
And they listen and sigh, with downcast eye,

Of the weary years that went dragging, dragging by.
But joyous, now, the fleet hours speed away,
As homeward bound the trim ship makes her way.

*   *   *   *   *

Land ho!   Afar, like a vision on his sight,
And the home-circling skies seem smiling with delight.
And a kiss in every breeze seems his waiting heart to
   cheer,
As he thinks of wife and children, and the old home-
   stead dear.
The friendly land grows nearer, soon the city spires nod.
And he wipes away a tear, as he kneels to thank his
   God.
In the harbor safe at last is the anchor nimbly cast,
And the weary days of waiting seem forever past.
A light bark, ripple-rocked, bears him safely to the
   strand ;
He seems a youth again, as he treads the glittering sand.
Homeward, joyously, alone he wends his way,
Which, the nearer 't is approached, brings a spirit of
   dismay—
A cold, forbidding air seems the premises around ;
No fond familiar essence says his loved ones here are
   found.
The dark forebodings thicken, as he meets a stranger
   there,

And he asks for wife and children, as he lays his troubles bare.

"Ha, ha! he, he! You 're the man the world would see.
Your family are scattered; this mansion belongs to me.
Look ye, sons and daughters, here 's the man who to see
the world sailed—
By a tempest on the ocean, his voyage was curtailed—
Seeking home and friends, a beggar now returned,
Will find himself rejected by former friends, and
spurned."

"Dear friend, that can not be; we had myriad friends,
not few,
And of that swarming myriad, sure many would prove
true.
I will seek my beauteous wife among the friends of
yore,
Cherished still, as when I left my native shore."

"Your wife? You 'll find her yonder, in that weather-
beaten cot."

There, sure enough, oh, sad to tell, he found the wife he
sought;
He clasped her to his weary heart; so wept the riven
pair—
Happy e'en thus to meet, though weighted each with
care;
She bowed with unused labor, forsaken and forlorn—
Striving for her daily bread, of every blessing shorn.

He found his sad-eyed children, neglected and toil-
worn—
Insults and privation were the burdens they had borne.
" Call back thy smiles, dear wife," he said ; " Glad tid-
ings I 've in store ;
For I come not back a beggar from off that foreign
shore.
Here, hidden in the folds of this ragged coat I wear,
Are gems enough to crown thee a three times millionair.
Call, call our sons and daughters into a princely home,
With sumptuous banquets spread beneath its sheltering
dome.
Our reunion we will celebrate with thankfulness and
mirth,
Recalling hope and pleasure around the family hearth ;
The vile summer friends, who fled and cut you with dis-
dain,
In our future opulence, we will not know again."

SPRING FLOWERS.

While the lily buds were sleeping
    In the month of March,
Came a snow-drop slyly peeping ;
    Her dark spears green as larch.

I, the earliest of flowers, said she,
    Must wake the crocus up,
The daisy and the violet,
    And then the lily cup.
The hyacinth, with sweet perfume,
    Must cheer us in the May,
While we wait the buttercup
    To brighten our array.
Huzza for our hardy band of flowers,
    That come e'er the wintry chills are past;
The harbinger of many sunny hours,
    Freed from winter's bonds at last.

LINES TO A PICTURE—THE YOUNG CHE-VALIER.

Young and beauteous chevalier,
You sit your steed without a fear,
And in your beauty seem to smile;
I fear you will my heart beguile.
With your little curly pate
Decked in plumes of high estate;
From your looks I think you 'd rate
Among the greatest of the great;

Or at least at beauty's shrine
The meed of beauty would be thine.
Where did you get that pony rare,
Which you with whip and rein ensnare?
I am sure its every form is grace;
Oh, how I'd like to see it pace!
Or how I'd like to take a ride,
With you, young chevalier, by my side.
You little rogue, why do n't you speak?
You look so brave, and yet so meek;
You vex me so, I've a notion to
Pull off your little buckled shoe.
Little beauteous, smiling boy,
Picture of innocence and joy,
Pray doff thy jaunty cap of blue,
While I bid thee an adieu.

LINES TO THE OCEAN.

Roll on, thou dark mysterious main,
But thy might I ne'er shall praise again,
Though thy mountain waves may towering lift
And dash their spray from cliff to cliff,
I ne'er shall sing in praise of thee,

Nor call thee mighty, grand, nor free ;
For thou didst hurl beneath thy wave
One that was lovely, true and brave.
Hidden 'neath thy waves forever,
My only beauteous fair haired brother ;
My father's hope, my mother's pride :
For him I gladly would have died.

Ah ! I shall smile no more on thee,
Thou wild and treacherous sea ;
I will hear no more of thy jeweled store ;
Thou hast a stolen pearl on thy shelly floor.
A gem of earth thou hast hidden below,
Where monsters sport and seaweeds grow.
Oh, ocean ! so cruel, forever untamed,
The good and true 'mong thy victims are named ;
Why yield ye not up our treasure, I pray,
That ye have hidden 'neath thy waves away ?
For we must scorn thy beauty and power forever,
While in the vales of thy deep lies my fair haired
    brother.

LIFE EVER CHANGING.

Twilight shadows murmur,
Heed the dying day ;

Every golden sunbeam
　Needs must pass away.
When the sun in splendor
　Seeks his western home,
The stars in bounden duty
　Gild the dusky dome.

So it is each flow'ret
　Blossoms in the glade,
Where it buds in beauty ;
　It must also fade.
Changing, ever changing,
　This our life we view ;
Year on year is ranging,
　Yet life is ever new.

Twilight shadows murmur,
　Days must pass away ;
Call not back the moments,
　Morn brings another day.
Then with cheerful singing
　Attune the heart to praise ;
For 't is wrong to murmur
　Of God's mysterious ways.

LOST BOY.

I have lost my child—a little golden-haired,
Blue-eyed boy—the light of home—its life and joy.
Oh, tell me, have you seen him anywhere—
This little cherub, with sunny hair,
With laughing eyes, and a dimple in his chin?
How I idolized the boy! I hope it was no sin.
It was long, long ago, when I lost my baby boy;
I have sought him every-where, and my life has lost its
    joy.
Tell me, stranger, have you seen him anywhere?
Just five years old was he, in his beauty all so rare.
Year after year goes flitting by, I'm old and feeble
    growing,
And yet I must not rest—ah, no, I must be up and
    going.
Postman, wandering every-where,
Have you seen a lost boy, with blue eyes and sunny
    hair?

POSTMAN.

Woman, I once knew a lost boy, just five years old,
His eyes the color of the skies, his hair like yellow gold;
But 'twas many years ago; to manhood now he's
    grown;

Should his mother find him now, no doubt she would
disown.
When lost you your life and joy,
In this lovely cherub boy?

WOMAN.

Ah, 't was twenty years ago, and my hair is white as
snow,
And there's wrinkles on my cheek and brow ;
He would not know his mother now—
My lost, my cherub boy!

POSTMAN.

Woman, just twenty years ago, my mother called me
cherub boy;
I was her life her light, her joy,
I wandered from my home, one day—
Wandered afar in wanton play ;
Since then, no mother's love I've known.
Mother, do not your son disown ;
I am thy long lost truant boy!

WOMAN.

No, no! it can not be! You, a man so rough and hale!
Wert thou my child, I must still bewail
My lost babe, my cherub boy!

POSTMAN (*presents his son*).
My mother lost in thee I see;
Mother, my child shall plead for me.
Here is my son, just five years old,
With azure eyes, and hair like gold.
Plead with your grandma, precious one,
That she may own her long lost son.

MOTHER (*clasps the child to her bosom*).
Thy son! 'T is mine—my long lost child!
It was I his infant years beguiled.
Found! Found at last! Oh, joy! Oh, joy!
My long lost, golden-haired, blue-eyed boy!

SONG OF THE BROOKLET.

Ripples gay were playing
   O'er a purling, silver stream,
And all the while were saying,
   Life is but a transient dream.

O'er pearly shells and pebbles,
   Still lightly they sped on,
Bursting into bubbles,
   With light and joyous song.

In the song they murmured,
In a cadence light and free,
We know our bounden duty
Is to swell the lakes and sea.

And though our might is feeble,
Union makes us strong;
Each little wandering streamlet
Joins in our matin song.

SUNSHINE AND SHADOW.

Strange are the passions that play round the heart,
And bring out the feelings of sadness and joy;
Dark are the shadows that fall round our pathway,
And mix all our pleasures with bitter alloy;
Yet we will murmur not, life is so queer,
Full many the blessings, our pathway to cheer;
While beauties cluster round, let us be gay,
Chasing the dark, gloomy shadows away.
Life is checkered, brilliant, and gray,
Sunshine and shadows disputing the way;
The orient glow lingers not long in the sky,
The storm cloud, in grandeur, as quickly speeds by;
Dark, gloomy night is succeeded by day,

Which bursts from the east in glittering array;
Sunshine and clouds make beauty complete,
And the bitter of life makes the sweet seem more sweet.

THE RAINBOW.

There is a banner unfurled in the sky,
No banner of empire, with its beauties, can vie;
Its colors are azure, and purple, and gold,
And often, quite often, other colors unfold.
It spans the broad dome of the heaven's light,
And millions admire its tintings bright;
When electric elements battle in air,
And thunders roll, and lightnings glare.
When the strife of the clouds in tranquillity cease,
'Tis then 'tis unfurled, 'tis the emblem of peace;
The clouds roll away, and thunders retreat,
Light sunbeams hasten the victory to greet.
From the misty heavens bends the beautiful bow,
Overarching the earth with rubied glow,
Its colors all blending sheds brightness around,
'Tis the bow of promise, so long renowned;
Its duties fulfilled, it fades from our sight,
Leaving earth brilliant in golden sunlight.

OLD FOGY AND YOUNG AMERICA.

(A Farce, designed for Beginners or Home Theatricals.)

DRAMATIS PERSONÆ.

OLD FOGY.

MANDY JANE, wife of Old Fogy.

YOUNG AMERICA, young son of Old Fogy and Mandy Jane.

ACT I.

SCENE 1.—Room in Old Fogy's residence. Old Fogy seated in arm-chair. Mandy Jane, switch in hand, is about to chastise Young America. Old Fogy interferes.

Old Fogy. Mandy, spare that child; a little wild he may be,

But a smarter boy of ten you never see;

And the exact image of his daddy, I declare,

His nose, his eyes, and e'en his hair;

I say, Mandy, the smartest boy that e'er was born;

Just hear the little shaver toot that horn.

Mandy Jane. Yes, 'tis toot, toot, from morn to night;

He begins his tricks before 'tis yet light.

I should think he was a little wild,

And I'le not spare the rod, and spile the child.

What his next trick will be, 'tis imposserble to tell,

And I'le tan his little hide, an tan it well.

Yestermorn, my satin skirt he took to make his boat a sail,

And stripped the ribbons from my hat to make his kite a tail.

Old Fogy. Wall now, that was a brilliant ideer, that ere;

He's an inventive little genus, I declare.

He's bound to hev a glorious fate,
He'l be a second Washington, or Alexander great.
He'l make a stir in this ere world, some day;
And that, too, before we both are gray.

Mandy Jane. Gray, gray, I feel tricolored now;
Mottled green and blue, with forty wrinkles on my brow.
He keeps my emotions tossin up and down, like a toy bal-
    loon;
Till I am quite as shaky as a fiddle out of tune.
From the depths of despair to the rafters of bliss,
When the little urchin begs forgiveness with a kiss.

Young America. I bet on dad; dad, you're O K,
Pull down your vest, an tell mam to golong away.
Tell her to dry up, that's a brick;
Tell her her gab is a wag too sleek.
You're a bully boy, dad; a brick of a chap;
You're a number one team, and nary a sap.

Old Fogy. Just hear the little chit chatter Latin,
Glib as any priest at matin;
See the advantage of free education,
The bone and siney of the nation.
The boy is most too smart to thrive;
I'me feared he'l not reach manhood's state alive. [Young
    America mews like a cat.]
Just hear that, too, his powers of imitation are wondrous.
Mandy, you mus be keerful of that boy,
He's destined to bring us both fame and joy. [Young
    America barks like a dog.]
There's another sample of his cuteness,
Such wit is prognostic of true greatness. [Young Amer-
    ica crows like a cock.]

Mandy, did you ever hear the like o' that?
Mimics a dog, a cock, a cat.
Sonny, come here an talk to daddy,
Like a darling little laddie. [Enthusiastically to Young
America. Young America whistles the call of the
bob-white.]
You, George Washington, you Napoleon, you Alexander
the great,
Come here, I want to pat your little pate. [Young Amer-
ica growls.]
Mandy Jane, I'me quite astonished, I declare,
Such powers of imitation are wondrous rare.
[To Young America.] Life of my life, soul of my soul,
come here.
Your daddy waits your rogueish kiss to cheer.
    Young America. Bah, pull down yer vest.
    Old Fogy. Wall, sonny, I haint wore no vest this ere
    many a day;
When the weather gets warm, I lays my vests away.
    Young America. You're a ticket.
    Old Fogy. No, sonny, I give you the last ticket I had,
    a week ago;
A yaller Democratic ticket, dont you 'member—haint it so?
    Young America. You bet.
    Old Fogy. No, sonny, I never bet; I think it wrong;
But I sometimes vent my hopes in patriotic song. .
    Young America. Hurrah, hear the governor.
    Old Fogy. No, sonny, I haint heard the governor yet;
When he made his nogeral speech, the day was wet;
And what with rumatiz and gout,
I very seldom can get out. [Old Fogy falls asleep in his
chair.]

Young America. Old Fogy collapsed, now for fun. [Gets
a pole, and block for lever, and gives the chair a lift.]
Old Fogy. [Waking in affright.] Mandy Jane, there's
bin another earthquake, surely,
Or else my nerves are getting poorly.
Frisco is shook up agin, I guess;
These quakes are rather common, I confess.
   Young America. Governor, I think I know what it was.
Old Fogy. What, thou darling little dove?
What, thou gift of Him above?
   Young America. One of those big mountains in the
moon tumbled out.
Old Fogy. Thou guileless cherub of thy sire,
Thy innocence can never tire.
   Young America. Daddy, how do you suppose I learned
to be so innocent?
Old Fogy. Innocence, my son, is inborn, not bred;
And, like genius, is to heaven wed,
And angels guard the innocent.
   Young America. Then about forty angels must guard
you, daddy.
Old Fogy. And guard they not my little sprite,
With spirits all so feather-light?
   Young America. No, they know better than to guard me.
Old Fogy. Why so, thou little oracle,
Destined to be historical?
   Young America. They know I want some quill feathers.
Old Fogy. So wise, I comprehend thee not,
Thou little Solomon, thou wisdom dot.
   Young America. They have wings, have they not?
Old Fogy. Wings they have, to enfold and guard
Pilgrims on life's journey hard.

Young America. Well, they know I'de take their quill
feathers.

Old Fogy. Stop, dont be sacriligious, boy ;
Thy fancy hath imbibed alloy ;
All holy things thou must revere,
And God, and heaven, and angels fear.
You'le be a good boy, will you not?
And fear your Maker as you ought?
And curb the impious thought, or hand,
When speaking of aught in the better land ?

Young America. Yes, I guess.

Mandy Jane. [Addressing son.] Say, sir ; Yes, sir.

Young America. Yes, sir ; Jolly cur.

Old Fogy. His tongue is so prolific of words,
I think he'l make an orator.

Young America. Yes, daddy, I'le make a reconorter.

Old Fogy. Hear that pun, Mandy ?
His wit is always glib an handy.

Young America. Now, daddy, limber your pegs and
skedaddle,
And I'le make you a speech ; so git up and straddle.

Old Fogy. Mandy Jane, if you understand his latin, I
wish you would explain.
That I can not understand the boy, kind of goes agin the
grain.

Young America. Now, daddy, hear me spout ;
Fourth of July will soon be out,
And I must rouse the patriotism of the nation,
To a rousceing celebration.
First give me a rag, and dabble it in indigo,
And streak it with polk-berry juice,
Tack Jupiter, Mars, Hershell, Venus, Saturn,

And eight big comets in the corner ;
Plant this startling banner on a ten pounder,
Blow the flute, and beat the drum,
To the tune of Yankee Doodle,
Accompanied by the crackling of a thousand shooting
    crackers.
Then if Russia, Johny Bull, or any other noodle,
Looks slantwise and says,
What young monster's that comeing ?
Pull down your brows, and say : Be wary, gentlemen, that's
    Young America.

ACT II.

Scene 2.—Parlor of Old Fogy's residence. Old Fogy and Mandy
    seated in easy chairs. Enter Tabitha and Ebineezer, daugh-
    ter and eldest son of Old Fogy.

Tabitha. Papa, mine, we are going to have a tableau
this evening.

Old Fogy. Now, Tabitha, you know I am opposed to
blows. You know the gospel injunction. "If they smite
thee on one cheek, turn to them the other." And tap
blows might soon turn to hard blows.

Tabitha. A *tableau*, a *tableau*, papa, dear.

Old Fogy. Never associate with any thing low, Tabitha,
leave the low to the low, be high minded always. I'me
afeared society's gittin a little loose.

Ebineezer. Why, yes, governor, it has been emancipated.

Old Fogy. [Aside.—Emancipated, emancipated, I suppose that's dutch for beheaded.] [Aloud.]—Its bin beheaded, has it, I thort so, but ye better be keerful for all

that, or it will behead you; some creeters bite arter ther heds are off. Rattlesnakes fer instance.

Ebineezer. That reminds me, governor, that you old fogys are some on fish and snake stories. So I move you tell us a snake story.

Tabitha. I second the motion.

Old Fogy. A snake story, ha, ha. Wall I dont mind telling you a snake story, pervided ye postpone them blows ye were speakin on.

Tab. and *Eb.* [At once.] We promise to postpone the tableau.

Old Fogy. Wall, while I was a sojerin in the Mexican war, down on the Rio Grande, I seed plenty o' snakes. My old comrade, Jem Brown, was orful feered o' snakes. He was that feered that he kept his hed continally bobbin like a duck, fust one side and then tother, a peekin fer snakes. Wall, one day we hed bin out on the scout an were about tired out; so seein a cool lookin spot close to the roadside, with a restful lookin log, about twenty foot long and two and a half foot in circumference, we concluded we'de stop thar and rest. So, takin out our lunch o' venison and corn-dodgers, Jem sot down on that ere log. Immegiately that ere log commenced wrigling; then the leetle eend ris up sudden like, an sent Jem flyin like a kite, and out of the other eend two eyes an a tongue, a blazin and a hissin like mad. That ere log were a big snake. Jem picked himself up, give one look at the creeter, and started runnin like a hare, and that tarnal snake arter him; an the're runnin yit; that's nigh onto thirty years ago.

Mandy Jane. Well, some benevolent body better hev some catnip tea ready for him when he do stop.

Ebineezer. I should prescribe a dose of assifœdita, to take the wind out of him.

Tabitha. Brother, dear, I am afraid there will be no wind left in him, and he will die for want of breath.

Ebineezer. Right, sister mine, people do sometimes die for want of breath. Governor, is not that stretched a little?

Old Fogy. Wall, I guess he's purty well stretched by this time.

Ebineezer. Father, you never told a lie, did you?

Old Fogy. What, sir! such a question to your father! Have I reared you from infancy to manhood, 'culcatin lessons of honesty and truth, to be questioned thus in my old age? Hev I not told yer agin and agin bout the story of George Washington an his little hatchit, that ye might know how I reverence truth?

Ebineezer. True, true, I beg your pardon, but in emulating George Washington you have gone quite as far as he, I fear, and done the mischief with your little hatch—it.

Old Fogy. Wall. son, we'l never loose by tryin to emerlate the good an grate.

Ebineezer. True, and what can not be accomplished by emulation can generally be accomplished by a little hatch—it.

Old Fogy. [Addressing Tabitha.] Tabitha, you've lost the bows ofen, yer har, an the're sprawlin all over yer frock.

Tabitha. Why, papa mine; that the last agony.

Old Fogy. The last agony! Oh, my gracious! I hope it's nothin ketchin, Tabitha?

Tabitha. Yes, papa, I confess they are awful catching.

Old Fogy. Well, hev them disinfected immigiately.

Tabitha. Too late, papa. I know of several young jentlemen already affected.

Old Fogy. From them agony bows?

Tabitha. Well, yes; the bows are very catching, and I am a very taking young lady, you understand, and the young jentlemen have already succumbed, and are badly smitten.

Old Fogy. If its your fault, Tabitha, I'le foot all the doctor bills.

Tabitha. It certainly is my fault, and I am afraid you will have to foot some bills.

Old Fogy. Mandy Jane, what do yer think o' that. Here's Tabitha taggin round catching things on her frock.

Mandy Jane. Well, then, she's a vixen, and desarves to hev her ears well boxed, an I've a good mind to do it.

Old Fogy. No, no, Mandy Jane, member she was a sweet little innercent onct.

Mandy Jane. Yes, but I'me afeared she's outgrowed it.

Ebineezer. Governor, allow me to explain. You misunderstand this daughter of yours. By " the last agony " she means that her ribbons are arranged after the latest fashions, and are pretty; consequently very catching or charming to her fashionable beaux, and being a very fascinating young lady herself, several young jentlemen are already in love with her, or are smitten, as she terms it, and if she gets married I guess you will have to foot some bills.

Old Fogy. Ha, ha, that's a good one. Mandy Jane, I'm afeared we'l have to acknowledge our young'uns are too smart fer us.

*Mandy Jane.** Yes, an they orter hev some o' there

smartness taken out o' them ; when I was young we were not allowed to be peert an smart afore our elders.

Old Fogy. Yes, Mandy Jane, but times are changed; ye heard Ebineezer say awhile ago that society had bin beheaded.

Mandy Jane. Wall, all I've got to say about it is, that they clipped off the wrong eend ; it orter been curtailed.

Old Fogy. Mandy Jane, yer right. When onct a thing git its hed off, it aint much account arterwards ; but it might a bin curtailed, an then if it dident whop right, it could a bin re tailed, yer see.

Mandy Jane. Yes, but dont let on, father ; its danger-ous. If onct they git the ideer it orter bin curtailed, they'l go an whack its tail off yit, and then ther'ed be nothin left, fer society were always like a wiggler, all hed an tail.

Old Fogy. Yes, Mandy Jane ; an between you an me, we might as well prepar to go up in a balloon, fer they've already gan whackin at its tail.

Mandy Jane. Father, it will break my heart to do that. I've saved the nicest punkin seed to plant next year.

Old Fogy. Take yer punkin seed with yer, Mandy Jane, and put in my fishin line ; there's nothin like bein pre-pared when yer go up in a balloon.

[Ebineezer in the meantime sews on a sewing-machine.]

[A knock at the door. Enter Aunt Jerusha, an old-fashioned old maid, with her reticule, bottle of salts, and knitting.]

Aunt Jerusha. Good evenin, folks, I jist called to see how ye were all gittin along. This is an amazin streak o' wet weather we're havin, and its makin a powerful lot o' sickness. Sister Jane's oldest boy's got the flewrisy, an 'tother one's got the brownsketers, and Mrs. Hook's got the

rumatiz, and Mrs. Hook says the doctor says Mr. Crank's
got the inafrenzy, and sed he shud tak a foot-bath three
times a day, and drink cyan-pepper tea. An thar's Sally
Jane's twins are gettin the hoopin-cough, an the baby's
got the measles, an what, with nussin and watchin the sick,
I are about down sick myself. I had sich amazin pains in
my hed last nite I thort sure I had inflation of the brain.
I called in Greer, that young flirt of a doctor (I don't believe he's got half sence), an I told him I thort I had inflation of the brain. He sed, no, it were more likely I had
sofenin of the brain ; but he said he knew a heap of folks
who were sufferin with inflation of the brain. He sed it
were s rt o' big bug disease, an mostly tacked the cod-
fish arristocracy. He sed its symptoms were mostly peert-
ness and puffupedness, an he tole me to bathe my hed in
hot water—as hot as I could bar it—an hot water bandages
on my hed till the pain quit, an not a bit of physic nor any
kind of medercine did he order. I was that disgussed I
come near orderin him outen the house. But, howsome-
ever, thinks I, hot wat r's cheap, an I dun as he tole me, an
sure enough my hed quit, but I guess it were merely accerdental. I seed him this mornin, an I axed him dident he
think I was thretened with a tact of parlysis of the brain.
He sed, no, I only had a tact of nerwus-hedake. Nerwus-
hedak! The ideer. I tole him it run in our family to hev
important diseases or none at all, an he needent try to
make me think such a triflin thing ailed me. He gave me a
peercin, sarchin look, and ses he, Aunt Jerusha I believe
I kin trust you with a secret. Mind now, ses he, you're
not to tell any one, but atween you and me, says he, you
have very serious symptoms of inflation of the brain.
There! said I, I knowed it ; I knowed it. And now doctor,

sed I, I want some o' the strongest medercine you can put up. Yes, sed he, I wont delay. We'l stop at Eli's drugstore. Mr. Eli has just got some powerful drugs from the East Ingies. Well, we stopped, an he axed Mr. Eli could he spare him about a quart of magnescyou, or something like that. I axed him did he call it mayigreascyou. He sed that were a secret knowed only to the fraternity, an he would not dar diwulge sich a important secret. Mr. Eli sed he could let him hev a peck if he wanted it. He sed, no, a quart would do. It took about a hour to put em up in doce papers. He said take a powder six times a day. I made him take a ten-dollar bill right thar. He dident want to take it, bein we were old frens and nabors, but, ses I, doctor when one comes right plump down with the truth about a important disease as you did I feel like payin for it, and here's the powders I hev to take [displaying a basketfull]. That proves somethin very important ails me. Inflation of the brain he sed. I knowed it; I knowed it; oh, dear, dear! I do feel so bad, an oh! I have got sich a palpertation right in my region, oh, my!

Ebineezer. [Here Ebineezer presents a dress to Tabitha.] Here, sister, see what industry can accomplish. I have made you a dress beruffled and tucked in the very latest style.

Aunt Jerusha. Mercy, a young man making a frock fer a gal! Oh, heavens, did I ever think I'de live to see the like of that! My salts, my smellin salts. [Faints away.]

Ebineezer. [Ebineezer rings the bell and calls for salt.] Salt, salt, bring some kitchen salt, quickly as possible.

[Enter servant with salt; Ebineezer receives the salt, and sprinkles Jerusha.]

Ebineezer. If the old creature wants to be salted, I can

salt her. The old fossil ought to have been salted down long ago.

Aunt Jerusha. [Reviving.] My salts, my smellin salts. [Tabitha hands her her bottle of salts. She revives.]

Aunt Jew. What is the matter? What have you dun? What is this white stuff all over my best gown?

Ebineezer. Aunt Jew, you just had one of your spells of inflation of the brain, and in your delirium cried frantically to besalted down.

Aunt Jew. Oh, my, has it come to this; salted down alive; oh, dear, dear!

[A knock at the door; enter Miss Dr. Glint, a modern old maid; she bows to the company.]

Miss Dr. Glint. Good morning, friends, [Stands at a distance, eyeing Aunt Jew. with her eye-glass.] Ho, ho; what have we here?

Ebineezer. A specimen of the lower silurian.

Miss Dr. Glint. Ah, a pretty good sized mollusk; hope you will donate it to our natural history collection, such a specimen should be preserved; but it appears animated.

Aunt Jew. You needent talk in French, dearies, I shant be frightened, I am perfectly resigned; the doctor says I have a very important disease, an we all have to die some time. I hev tried to do my duty, an when my summons comes I hope to go where "the wicked cease from troubling, and the weary are at rest."

Ebineezer. We hope so, too. However, I think I should fare better if the quotation read differently, say: Where the weary cease from troubling, and the wicked are at rest.

Aunt Jew. No, dearie; "No rest for the wicked," and "the way of the transgressor is hard." You know the good book says that.

Ebineezer. Well, I suppose that means hard cash. The way of the transgressor is hard cash these times sure.

Aunt Jew. Oh, my, I do feel so missible.

Miss Dr. Glint. My dear friend, allow me to prescribe for you; it shall be gratis.

Aunt Jew. Gratis; be that any thing like grits? If it be, I wont take the bomerball stuff.

Miss Dr. Glint. Oh, no; I only mean I shall prescribe free of charge.

Aunt Jew. What rights have ye to be scribin fer sick folks.

Miss Dr. Glint. The very best of rights; I am a graduate of the very highest medical college in the land; have received my diploma, and am a practicing physician; also an exquisite surgeon and dentist; and if ever you should suffer a broken limb, just send for me, and I shall amputate or set, just as the case requires, with the greatest skill.

Aunt Jew. You dont say so! Heaven deliver me! Mandy Jane, fer mercy's sake lend me yer pertection, and send that creetur away. I'me astonished at yer fer havin her sociatin with yer innercent chillern.

Mandy Jane. Oh, well, she's the grandarter of Josier Rule, one of our oldest an bes frens. You member Josier Rule?

Aunt Jew. Tew be sure I do; it cant be poserble this are his grandarter. To think any of his kin shud come to this. What are the wurl a comin to?

Miss Dr. Glint. Coming to perfection, my friend. [Aside to family—I must ignore our friend's aspersions on my character on account of her extreme verdancy.]

Tabitha. Kind.

Ebineezer. Magnanimous.

Miss Dr. Glint. [Aside—I shall insist on taking a diagnosis of her ailment, and we shall have some amusement.]

Tab. and *Eb.* Do, do.

Miss Dr. Glint. My friend, where is the pain that troubles you so much?

Aunt Jew. [Laying her hand on her breast.] Right here in my region.

Miss Dr. Glint. [Winks at family and says:] Quite an unexplored region.

Aunt Jew. Explode region, oh dear! I wont explode, will I?

Miss Dr. Glint. Not at all; there is more danger of your becoming fossilized. Do you have excruciating pains?

Aunt Jew. If you mean have I pains from ateing screws, I tell you, no. I guess I hev got more sence than to be screw ateing.

Miss Lr. Glint. I wish to inquire minutely into the cause of your indisposition.

Aunt Jew. Wall, my inside dispersition are just as good as my outside dispersition are.

Miss Dr. Glint. You have never been dissipated, have you?

Aunt Jew. I dont know, for sure. They say my great great gran father were a Dutchman, an they say he had a good pate on him; so I *spose* Ime pated; but I dont know.

Ebineezer. Oh, she has got a head on her; "that's what's the matter."

Miss Dr. Glint. In other words, were you ever fast?

Aunt Jew. I cud run purty fast when I was a gal.

Miss Dr. Glint. Plainer yet. Were you ever inclined to be wild?

Aunt Jew. If you mean skittish, I never felt skittish till I seed you, an hearn you say ye wer a doctor, surgin, etc.

Ebinezer. Ho, ho, Doctress Glint; she turns the tables on you.

Miss Dr. Glint. You do not believe in woman's rights, then?

Aunt Jew. No, no! May the Lord forgive me if ever I believe in ooman's rights. Do you believe in ooman's rights?

Miss Dr. Glint. To be sure I do. Does not my profession proclaim that?

Aunt Jew. Help! help! Mercy! mercy! Ile be dewoured alive!

Mandy Jane. [Rushing up to Aunt Jew.] What is it, Aunt Jew? What is the matter?

Aunt Jew. O, Mandy Jane, I need pertection, I do; call yer ole man, I need pertection. This ere woman a woman's rights woman, she is. I mus get outen these diggins, I mus. I feel too orful weak to walk, but if you'l just stop a wagin or a dray, Mandy Jane, I'le go hum.

[A knock at the door. Enter Hezekiah, an old fashioned old bachelor.]

Hezekiah. Good mornin, folks.

Aunt Jew. [Aside—I will stay awhile longer; Hezekier is sich an innercent feller he'l need pertection.] [Advancing, shakes hands with Hezekiah.] How do ye do, Hezekier? How is yer mar?

Hezekiah. Purty well, but she's got the toothache.

Aunt Jew. How's yer par, Hezekier?

Hezekiah. Purty well, but *he's* got the toothache.

Aunt Jew. How's yer sister, Hezekier?

Hezekiah. She's purty well, but she's got the toothache, too.

Miss Dr. Glint. My dear sir, you seem to have bad teeth in your family.

Hezekiah. Yes, we do, an I had an orful toothache, too, last nite.

Miss Dr. Glint. Sir, why do you not have your teeth fixed?

Hezekiah. O, ther not woth fixin, ther all bad.

Miss Dr. Glint. Sir, here is my card; that is the number of my office. If you will just call at my office, I will guarantee to extract all of your teeth and furnish you a full new set (upper and lower) for twenty dollars.

Hezekiah. Hey? what did yer say?

Miss Dr. Glint. I say I will remove your old teeth without pain, and furnish you a full new set for twenty dollars. Just let me look at your teeth a minute.

Hezekiah. Oh, no! No yer dont! I've hearn tell o' them docters who pull yer teeth all out; but they wont get no chance to try that ere game on me. I mus go.

Aunt Jew. [Pleading.] Oh, dont go yet, Hezekier; I'le pertect yer. How's yer Ant Hanner, Hezekier?

Hezekiah. She's purty well.

Ebineezer. Has she got the toothache?

Hezekiah. No, she haint got no teeth at all.

Ebineezer. Like Uncle Ned, "she's got no teeth for to eat the corn cake."

Hezekiah. Nor, nor bread nither; she has to sop all her wittles.

Aunt Jew. Give her my love, Hezekier, and tell her I'me knittin you a harnsome pair o' socks fer yer Chrismas gif.

Hezekiah. Yes'm.

Aunt Jew. Haint yer never goin to git married, Hezekier?

Hezekiah. Wall, I dont know; I'me kind o' skeered to.

Aunt Jew. What are ye skeered of, Hezekier?

Hezekiah. Oh, I dont know; but they say there's a heap o' them woman's rights women now-a-days.

Aunt Jew. So there be, Hezekier, an you need pertection.

Hezekiah. Yes, I do!

Aunt Jew. An I need pertection, I do; for thar's one o' them oomen's rights oomans right that.

Hezekiah. You dont say so? Take my arm, Jerusha.

Aunt Jew. Will you pertect me, Hezekier?

Hezekiah. · Yes, I will!

Aunt Jew. For life, Hezekier?

Hezekiah. Yes, I will!

Aunt Jew. Will ye send for the parson, Hezekiah?

Hezekiah. Yes, I will! You an me mus have pertection, we mus. [Timidly.] You'l pertect me, too, Jerusha?

Aunt Jew. To be sure I will, as long as I live.

Ebineezer. If you intend getting married immediately, allow me to send for the minister; and do get married here. We have not witnessed a wedding for some time, and it will certainly give us great pleasure to have you married here.

Hezekiah. I would jis as lief be married hure, if only my mar an par an my sister wer hure.

Ebineezer. I can send a carriage for your parents and sister.

Aunt Jew. But I haint got no weddin frock.

Hezekiah. An I orter hev on a white ves.

Ebineezer. Do not worry about that, Hezekiah. My barber and tailor will soon put you in fine trim.

Tabitha. And I, Aunt Jew, will arrange your toilit.

Ebineezer. Which minister would you prefer should perform the ceremony?

Aunt Jew. Parson Brown, to be sure.

Hezekiah. Yes, Parson Brown.

[Ebineezer rings for servant; enter servant.]

Servant. At your service, sir.

Ebineezer. [To servant.] Take the carriage immediately, and bring Parson Brown here as soon as possible; also Miss, Mrs., and Mr. Diddle. They must be here within the hour.

Servant. Your orders shall be obeyed. [Exit servant.]

Tabitha. Now, Aunt Jew, come to my dressing-room, and arrange your toilet.

Aunt Jew. Bein I'me so unprepared, I guess I'le hev to and be much obleeged to ye too.

Tabitha. Not at all Aunt Jew, and I shall be pleased to accommodate you. You have no idea how much a fashionable toilet will improve your appearance. [Exit Tabitha and Jerusha.]

Ebineezer. [Addressing Hezekiah.] Come with me, my dear sir; we will see about that white vest of yours. [Exit Ebineezer and Hezekiah.]

Old Fogy. Mandy Jane, I be jist struck dum, I be. Here's that ole young couple hev gon an popped the question right afore our eyes, an never axed our advice or nuthin. An to make it wus, all the giddlesome things put ther heds together an trumped up a weddin right under our very noses, an never sed may I. An we wont be invited to the weddin, Mandy Jane, bein its in our own house; but, as we've bin docile speckeltaters so fer, I spose they'l allow us to sit in the corner an medertate on ther imperdence till they git thru with it.

Mandy Jane. Father, dont say nothin ; my harts pretty nigh broke. To think Hezekier and Jerusha shud hev to git marryd to pertect one another. ∙ But thar is one conserlation, our own young'uns dont need pertectin? it seems they ken take keer o' themselves, an manage the rest o' makind besides.

Old Fogy. That's a fact, Mandy Jane, an atween you an me, we are a pretty well managed ole couple. But when a body gits ole an stiff in the jints, it dont do any good to git rambucksious. But we'l fix em, Mandy Jane, when we go up in a balloon. I cant help thinkin o' that plan o' ours ; what a conserlation that will be ; we'l soar above earth, an all its turmoils, and enjy the peace that passeth understandin. I'le have nothing in the world to do but to fish, Mandy Jane, and you can raise pumpkins.

[Re enter Ebineezer, Hezekiah, Tabitha, and Aunt Jew. Mrs. Dr. Glint plays the wedding march on piano. Hezekiah and Aunt Jew are so transformed by dress that they do not recognize one another. They all sit in silence until the wedding march is ended. Then Aunt Jew opens a door and calls Hezekiah.]

Aunt Jew. Hez—e—ki—errr, Hez—e—ki—errr.

[Hezekiah also opens a door and calls Jerusha.]

Hezekiah. Je—ru—sha, Je—ru—sha.

Ebineezer. Why the verds do n't recognize one another. Ladies and gentlemen, allow me to make you acquainted with Miss Jerusha Fanstock and Mr. Hezekiah Diddle.

Aunt Jew. Oh, Hezekiah, be that you ? What hev they did to you. [Clasps his hand.]

Hezekiah. Lookey here, young ooman, dont be too peert. I'me goin to git married to Jerusha to-nite, so jis stan back and dont come shinin round me so free like.

Aunt Jew. Oh, Hezekiah, dont yer know me?

Hezekiah. Look a here, young woman, dont come friskin roun me that a way. I'me goin to be marrid right away, so you're too late; an I tell ye I dont know ye, so stan away now.

Aunt Jew. Dont ye know yer Jerusha, Hezekier?

Hezekiah. Be you Jerusha?

Aunt Jew. [Plaintively.] Oh yes, Hezekiah.

Hezekiah. Well I be blarsted if ever I marry sich a rig. I mus go hum.

Aunt Jew. [Wildly.] Oh, no, Hezekier! Dont fersake yer Jerusha that a way. [Jew to Tabitha.] Take off this bomerball riggin. [Tabith removes the veil, wreath, and ribbons.] Now, Hezekier, you hev no objections to me now, hev ye?

Hezekiah. Yes, Jerusha, put up them cur-ruls, an put yer har in a hard knot behin yer hed, like a wise ooman. [Jerusha puts her hair tightly back in a knot,] Now ye look nateral. Are ye reddy to git marrid now, Jerusha?

Aunt Jew. I don't know, Hezekier, you look so strange like, I feel skeert. What hev ye done with yer purty long har, Hezekier?

Hez. Why that sap of a barber whacked it all off.

Aunt Jew. [Plaintively.] Let me stretch it a leettle, Hezekiah. I dont like to marry a strange looking man; an if ye will just sot down an let me stretch yer har down longer ye will look more like yourself.

Hez. Well, dont yer pull to hard, Jerusha. [She pulls his hair down, but it will not stay.]

Aunt Jew. Hezekier, yer har's got curley, and it wont

stay down. I must grease it. Folks cant ye spar me some ile?

Ebineezer. [I have never before known of a case where the hair-pulling commenced before marriage, and she seems expert at it, too, although she is a spinster. It is undoubtedly a herditary instinct, and in this case, though lying dormant for fifty years, is at once vitalized by the possession of a victim. Oil will undoubtedly bring relief to the poor dupe, so I hasten to the rescue.] Aunt Jew here is a bottle of hair-oil. [Gives Aunt Jew a bottle of oil.]

[Aunt Jew takes the bottle and oils his hair liberally, pulling it down in spikes round his head.]

Aunt Jew. [Lovingly.] Now, Hezekier, yer look more nateral like. [Gives one more good pull, and off comes a wig. She falls on her knees in prayer, and exclaims:] Merciful Father, forgive me for what I have did this day! Mercy, mercy! I hev scalped my best beloved one!

Hez. No yer haint, Jerusha; Ime soon as a fiddle yit. That sap of a barber clapped a shene on and tuk every single har ofen my hed till it looked like a hog's. An I told him plagued ef I'de git married without any har. So the little purp clapped a wig on my hed; and dont ye be gittin the hystericks Jerusha, for Ile swar Ime sound yet.

Aunt Jew. Mercy, mercy! Haint I kilt yer, Hezekier?

Hez. Not by a long short.

Aunt Jew. [Very severely.] Then ye mean to say ye are meerly a hypercrite, a totin roun false har on yer hed.

Hez. It are meerly accerdental, Jerusha. Ye would not hev me ketch my deth of cold, would ye? But if you say so we kin postpone the wedding till my har grows.

Aunt Jew. [Wildly.] No, no, Hezekier, a man without a hed are better than no man at all.

[A knock at the door. Enter Parson Brown. He shakes hands with the old folks.]

Parson Brown. How are you, brother? How do you do, sister? Allow me to congratulate, sister Fanstock; and you, brother Diddle, each in having found at last a congenial companion with whom to tread the journey of life. May joy accompany you to the heavenly gates.

[Old Fogy introduces his son to Parson Brown.]

Old Fogy. [Parson, this is my oldest son, Ebineezer.

Parson Brown. How do you do, young man? I saw you at our meeting Sunday, and I feel to be thankful that you are being drawn within the fold, where you may be hedged round about, and protected from the snares of the world. I hope you will give your heart to the Lord, young man, and be made to see your sinfulness.

Ebineezer. Beg your pardon, doctor, but you are certainly mistaken in my character. I have always felt remarkably innocent, and my heart has already been given to a young lady, as the Lord in his great wisdom intended it should be given.

Parson Brown. Tut, tut. How did our services impress you Sunday?

Ebineezer. Well, I was impressed with the idea that your's was a rampant religion.

Parson Brown. Exactly. As it should be. Are we not commanded to be zealous in all good works? Was that the only impression they gave?

Ebineezer. Well, no, I was more firmly impressed with the knowledge that the Great Creator, the God of heaven and earth, was a pretty well bossed God.

Parson Brown. [Addressing Old Fogy, anxiously.] My venerable brother has this young ever man been baptized?

Old Fogy. He was sprinkled.

Parson Brown. Ah, I think immersion would have been more beneficial to him.

[Enter Mr. Diddle, Sr., Mrs. Diddle, and Miss Diddle. They bow to the company. Mr. Diddle addresses Hezekiah.]

Mrs. Diddle. Look a here, Hezekier, they tell me ye are a goin to git married. You, scarcely weaned yet, and a goin to git married. I wont have it, Hezekier!

Hezekiah. Well, mar, I couldn't stan it any longer.

Mrs. D. [Severely]. Couldn't stan what.

Hez. Why, mar, you know, whenever a gurrel come about, you made me shet my eyes and run and hide.

Mrs. D. Well, that's the way a *nice* young man orter do.

Hez. Well, mar, I couldn't stan it. I hev always bin aflicted ever since I were a leetle boy.

Mrs. D. How hev ye bin aflicted?

* *Hez.* With a deep afection for the gurrels.

Mrs. D. [Severely, stamping her foot.] Well, why didn't ye shet yer eyes as I tole ye to?

Hez. Mar, it didn't do any good. I couldn't keep from peekin.

Mrs. D. Well, since ye will marry, why don't ye marry a young thing what ye can mannage?

Hez. Mar, I want some one to manage me, I do. The straight and narrer path I hev got to trod thru life, be so all fired narrer, I can't trod it, thout I hev ballust.

Mrs. D. Hezekier, ye are a lunertic; so get on yer straight-jacket as soon as yev'e a mind to.

Hez. [Joyously.] Come, Jerusha, let's git spliced right away. [Marriage Scene.]

[THE END.]